BEST FRIENDS FOREVER

ORCHARD

ORCHARD BOOKS
Carmelite House
50 Victoria Embankment
London EC4Y 0DZ
First published in 2018 in the United States
by Little, Brown and Company

This edition published by Orchard Books in 2018

A CIP catalogue record for this book is available
from the British Library.

ISBN 978 1 40835 647 0

1 3 5 7 9 10 8 6 4 2

Printed in Great Britain

Orchard Books
An imprint of Hachette Children's Group
Part of The Watts Publishing Group Limited
An Hachette UK Company
www.hachette.co.uk

www.hachettechildrens.co.uk

MIX
Paper from
responsible sources
FSC® C104740

The paper and board used in this book
are made from wood from responsible sources.

CHAPTER ONE

HIDE-AND-SEEK SURPRISES

It was almost spring and the Enchantimals were playing hide-and-seek.

Bree's fuzzy bunny ears poked up from behind a bush. They twitched and wiggled. She was listening for something. She was listening so closely that she didn't see the bushy red tail of a fox moving closer and closer.

"Gotcha!" exclaimed the fox-girl. Felicity had found her friend Bree!

Bree laughed as she hopped out of her hiding place. She pulled a leaf out of her long pink hair. "You're the greatest hide-and-seeker ever," she told Felicity. "I can't believe you found me so quickly!"

"Thanks, Bree," Felicity said. "But you're the only one I've found so far. Want to help me find the other hiders?"

"Does a bunny like carrots?" Bree grinned.

Beside Bree, Twist the bunny took a nibble from a carrot. "Uh-huh!" she agreed. She thumped her paws happily against the ground and began dancing with Bree. The Enchantimals each had a special connection with their besties. There were things they understood about each other that no one else did … and each pair had their own little dances and greetings.

"Come on," Felicity called. "Flick and the others must be around here somewhere."

They went further into the forest to look for their friends.

Meanwhile, Flick was still looking for a place to hide. Flick was Felicity's bestie and she knew she had to find a great hiding spot to outfox Felicity. She tried to wiggle into a hollow log but her bushy tail stuck out at the end of it. She noticed a butterfly watching her.

"Shhh!" whispered Flick. She scampered over to a boulder and crouched behind it. But her little red ears peeked over the rock. The butterfly fluttered over to her. "Hrumph! Voo zou tuu!" said Flick.

Where could she go? She looked all around the forest. She looked up into the trees. Then she looked down at the ground. Now that was an idea!

She began digging a hole with her front paws as fast as she could. She burrowed inside and pulled some leaves on top of herself. This was perfect! No one would notice her here, she thought. But the wind was gusting and blowing. The leaves whirled away into the trees. Now everyone would see her.

Flick grumbled. What was she going to do? A huge leaf blew into her face and stuck to her whiskers. Flick peeled

it away. It didn't look like any leaf she
had ever seen before in Wonderwood.
It shimmered green and purple. At its
centre was a black spot that glimmered in
the sunlight. It wasn't a leaf at all, Flick
realised. It was a feather. But what kind
of bird had feathers like this?

"Oooh ahh!" Flick exclaimed.
She wanted to show it to her friends,
especially her bestie, Felicity. Where was
everyone?

Forgetting all about finding the
perfect hiding spot,
Flick decided it was
time to start seeking.
This was turning
into a very different
kind of game!

CHAPTER TWO

SNIFFING OUT SECRETS

Felicity was following her nose. She sniffed carefully. "I think we're near Sage's hiding place," she whispered to Bree and Twist.

"Yeah," agreed Bree. "I can smell her perfume." Her little nose twitched as the skunk's special odour wafted through the air.

Twist the bunny coughed. That scent was strong!

"Phew!" Bree had to hold her nose.

Felicity sneaked over to a low leafy tree and pulled away a branch in the spot where the scent was strongest. But it wasn't Sage she found! It was Danessa.

Danessa's eyes were shut. "Don't move," she whispered to her bestie, Sprint the deer. "I think our camouflage is working …"

But it wasn't. Danessa shook her antlers when she realised she'd been discovered. Sprint nuzzled close to her.

"We've got to work on our hiding game," Danessa said to Sprint. They tapped their antlers together. It was their special greeting for each other.

Bree was confused. Why did they smell like skunks? "You guys don't wear perfume," she said.

Felicity was peering into the shadows. "Those skunks must be around here somewhere."

"No, we're not," said a voice.

Felicity laughed. "Hello, Sage! You just gave yourself away!" But where was the skunk-girl? Felicity still couldn't see her!

"Ha ha! Gotcha!" Sage laughed. She swung down from a branch above Felicity. When she landed, she held up a bottle of perfume and spritzed it into the air. "Ah! The sweet smell of a good trick!"

Danessa was impressed. "Well done, Sage."

"Another one of your crazy practical

8

jokes." Felicity grinned.

"Naaah." Sage shook her head, her black-and-white ponytail bouncing over her shoulder. "Just good hide-and-seeking!"

"OK," said Bree. "Who's left to find?"

"Well, we still haven't found Caper," Sage noted. Caper was her bestie.

"And Flick," added Danessa. "But good luck finding her. She always finds the best hiding places ..."

Just then, Flick came running towards the circle of girls. She was holding a strange feather in her mouth.

"Flick, why aren't you hiding?" Felicity asked.

Flick scampered into Felicity's arms. Her fur and Felicity's hair were exactly the same shade of orange. They wiggled their ears, greeting each other. "Oodah doodah ta!" Flick chattered, showing the others what she'd found.

"Wow!" Felicity was excited. "What a great find!"

A gust of wind whisked the feather out of Flick's paws.

"Whoa!" she exclaimed.

The feather twirled in the wind, shimmering and shining. As it gently floated down, Danessa caught it.

"It's a feather," she said. "But not like any feather I've ever seen before. I wonder who it belongs to!"

"Want to show us where you found this, Flick?" Felicity asked.

But Flick had been in such a hurry to find her friends that she couldn't remember where she'd come from. She

looked up one trail and down another.
Finally, she shrugged apologetically.
That's when the fox saw the butterfly.

"Felah!" Flick exclaimed, pointing
at it.

Felicity clapped her hands. "Perfect!
Butterflies know how to get just about
anywhere, don't they?"

The butterfly danced around the girls
before leading them deep into the forest.
At last they entered a clearing and Flick
spotted the hole that she had dug.

"Ooh da doo!" Flick announced.

"Great," answered Felicity. "Let's
start searching. Enchantimals, you look
high. Besties, you look low!"

Everyone spread out but Bree
became distracted by a leaf pile. She
took a big running jump and hopped

into it, giggling.

"Oooh!" exclaimed Twist with delight.

The friends were playfully hopping up and down when Twist saw another green-and-purple feather glimmering in a nearby leaf pile. She reached out with her paw and grabbed it.

"Eeeeawwwkkk!" squawked a voice. A little peacock emerged, rubbing his back end. Ouch! Someone had just pulled out one of his tail feathers!

Twist felt terrible. "Sawwy," she apologised.

Who was this strange bird? Twist had never seen one like him in all of Wonderwood.

CHAPTER THREE

BIRDS OF A FEATHER

A beautiful girl with bright purple hair and blue wings rushed through the trees to the clearing. "You OK, Flap?" she asked her bestie. A moment later she realised that a crowd of girls and their animals were staring at her.

"Oh!" she exclaimed in surprise. "Hello!"

Twist offered her the feather, looking

a little embarrassed.

"No worries. You can keep it," said
the new girl. "There's plenty more where
that came from!"

"Thank you," said Bree sweetly. "It's
beautiful."

"You can put it in your hair for
an extra touch of glamour," said the
girl, taking the feather from Twist and
sticking it in Bree's hair. "Stunning!"

Sage spritzed herself with a fresh dose
of perfume and stepped forward. "Hi, I'm
Sage," she said with a smile. "Do you live
around here?"

The new girl shook her head. "No,
and honestly, we don't even know where
'here' is. We come from Junglewood.
That's where we live. Lived." Her face
fell. She looked very sad.

"Isn't that at the far end of Everwilde?" asked Felicity.

"Yes, where it's nice and warm," said the girl. "But there was a huge windstorm and a tree fell on our home and we were swept away by the Babbling Brook and ended up down here and…" She looked around. "I don't even know quite where we are or if we are heading in the right direction to get back home again and I'm talking really fast aren't I? I become a little chatterbox when I'm nervous and I guess I'm nervous now because I don't know any of you but sometimes when I sing it helps me calm down so if you don't mind—"

The friends stared wide-eyed as the girl began squawking. Her peacock bestie covered his ears.

15

"La-la-la-la-la-la-LA!" the new girl shrieked. Her voice was horribly out of tune but that didn't stop her. She sang loud and long until she didn't have any more breath in her. "Ah," she sighed at last. "Much better."

No one knew what to say. Felicity wanted to make the girl feel welcome. So she stepped forward and introduced herself with a warm smile.

"Flick! Flick! Flick!" added her bestie.

"My name's Danessa!"

All the girls and their besties introduced themselves to the nervous girl to try to make her feel less uncomfortable.

The new girl smiled. "Nice to meet you all. We've never met woodland Enchantimals before. Just jungle ones. I'm Patter and this is my bestie, Flap."

Flap shyly hid behind Patter's legs. Patter put her wing around him. "He's still pretty upset that we had to leave Junglewood," she explained.

"I can see why," said Bree kindly. "I mean, a tree fell on your house."

Sage nodded. "And you were swept away by the Babbling Brook."

"Doesn't get much worse than that," Danessa agreed.

Flap shuddered at the memory. He clung to Patter's leg.

"We're glad you both ended up here in Wonderwood," Felicity told Patter.

"It's a really fun, forest-y place," Sage added.

"Over there is the town centre," Bree explained, pointing, "and over there is where we all live."

"Why don't we show you around?" Felicity suggested to Patter.

Patter looked uncertain. "I don't know," she said.

"You must be exhausted," Danessa realised. "Wonderwood is the perfect place to catch your breath while you figure out what to do next."

"Hmmm." Patter considered this. "That's not a bad idea. We are pretty tired. What do you think, Flap?"

The peacock was so tired. His blue eyes looked unsure. He shook his head.

Patter bent down to speak to him.

"These woodland

Enchantimals seem nice," she told
her bestie. "Besides, we've never been
anywhere outside of Junglewood. It could
be fun."

Flap knew that everyone was staring
at him. "Kay, kay," he said finally.

"Great!" Patter exclaimed.

Danessa was excited to show the new
girl around. "Come on, Sprint! Let's
show them the way!" She dashed off
through the trees.

"Whoa! She sure is fast," Patter was
impressed. "What kind of animal is she?"

Sage spoke up. "Doe."

"A deer," explained Bree.

"A female deer," Felicity added.

"Wow!" gushed Patter. Her new
friends seemed so wonderful. She couldn't
wait to learn more about them. She was

so excited that she didn't notice how
unhappy Flap was. His feathers dragged
on the ground as he followed the girls
and their besties to town.

CHAPTER FOUR

A LITTLE TEAMWORK

The gusty wind had brought down a tree. Its trunk had crushed the footbridge over the Babbling Brook. There was no way for the friends to cross to the village.

"Whoa!" said Sage, checking out the damage.

Felicity studied the stream. "The current looks pretty strong here." It would be too dangerous for the girls to wade across.

"Oh yes, we know," Patter agreed with her. "The Babbling Brook brought us here. Well, technically a big log on the Babbling Brook brought us here. One scary trip on those waters was definitely enough for us, right, Flap?"

Flap nodded.

"Well, it might have been scary," said Felicity, "but the Babbling Brook's waters carried you here safely to us."

"The Babbling Brook is so full of wonder," Danessa added softly.

Bree was gazing into the blue water. "I guess since she runs everywhere, she sees everything," she said thoughtfully.

"And when the time is right, she can show us things," Sage noted.

Felicity's eyes sparkled. "She's the all-knowing communicator of Everwilde!"

Patter was amazed. "Really? I had no idea. How do you know all this?"

"Felicity has a knack for communicating with her," Bree explained.

"The Babbling Brook can be a little choosy about who she chats to," said Sage.

Danessa wiggled her antlers excitedly. "Show her, Felicity!"

"Yeah, Felicity!" encouraged the others.

But Felicity shook her head. "Slow down, everyone! You know the Babbling Brook's enchantment isn't to be used willy-nilly. Her communications are precious gifts. Come on! Let's figure out how to get across so we can get on with our tour."

Bree was thinking. She loved solving problems and was really good at it. She had a plan. "My friends call me 'the Fixer'," she told Patter and Flap. "I'm the handiest bunny west of Craggy Peak Mountain."

Twist thumped her back paws in agreement. "Zou-zou, zou-zou!"

"We're gonna build a new bridge," Bree announced. "C'mon!"

She found the biggest rocks she could move and began rolling them towards the brook. She stacked the smaller ones on top of the bigger ones. The other girls all helped.

Sage was studying her work. "We need something that will hold these stones together," she said a moment later.

Bree grinned. "I got one word for you: SAP!"

"Brilliant!" Felicity exclaimed.

Sage and Caper began wagging their tails back and forth in a special signal. A moment later, a woodpecker flew down beside them.

As if it could understand exactly what they needed, it pecked at a tree until it'd created simple shovels out of wood chips for the girls to use. Then it pecked even harder at the trunk and a thin stream of sticky sap began to run out of the hole in the tree.

"Nature has the best glue ever," said Bree. "It's time to get sappy." She scooped up some sap with her new shovel and spread it across the tops of the stones. Then she stacked on another layer of rocks. It worked!

Patter and Flap were both impressed.
These girls were creative – and they knew
how to work together.

"Wow, what a team!" Patter
exclaimed. She and Flap began helping
out, too, and it wasn't long before the
stone bridge was done.

Bree looked at it, satisfied. "There you
go!" She sighed.

Twist held up a paw. "Look!"

An old tortoise was slowly crawling
towards the brook.

"I guess a few other
travellers will be using our
bridge, too," said Bree.

Sage bent down, picked
up the tortoise and gently
placed him on the other side.

It would have taken him all day to slowly crawl across on his own. "I just saved that guy, like, a month," Sage laughed.

Everyone joined in, including Patter. She liked these girls! What a surprising day this was turning out to be.

CHAPTER FIVE

FRIENDSHIP BLOOMS

As the girls entered the village, they passed an old cottage. The windows were broken. The paint was peeling. Vines had climbed up over the roof.

"What a sad-looking house," said Patter. "I bet it was beautiful once. Reminds me of …" It reminded her of her old house, but she didn't want to say that and upset Flap. "Never mind."

"No one's lived here for a long time" Felicity explained. "Kinda spooky, isn't it?"

Sage shrugged. "I don't know. It doesn't look that—"

"BOO!" A dark shadow was emerging from one of the windows.

"Ahh!" screamed the girls and their besties.

But it was just Caper. She giggled. She'd sneaked ahead to play a trick on everyone.

Sage shook her head. Her bestie was so good at practical jokes. "You got me again!" She laughed. "Honestly, I don't know where she gets it from."

Caper used her bushy black-and-white tail to brush the dust off her back. Then the two friends did their own version of a high five, using their tails. It was their special handshake, or tail-shake.

Felicity noticed that Patter was looking a little nervous. "Don't worry," she reassured the peacock-girl. "Our cottages aren't anything like this old place."

"Not at all!" Bree agreed. "They're way less fally-downy."

Ding-dong! Ding-dong! Ding-dong! The chimes of a bell rang from the village.

"Oh!" exclaimed Felicity. "It's already noon. I can't believe it!"

"Yay!" shouted all the other girls together, except for Patter. She wasn't sure what all the excitement was about.

"Today we start the countdown to the

Big Bloom!" explained Felicity.

"Oh! The Big Bloom!" Patter nodded.
"What's that?"

"Only the biggest, most important
celebration in Wonderwood," Sage
gushed.

"In three days the whole village will
celebrate the first day of spring!" added
Bree.

Patter smiled. Now she really did
understand! "The Big Bloom. Catchy."

"Hey, why don't you two celebrate the
Big Bloom with us?" Danessa suggested.
The deer-girl was always so thoughtful.
"You could stay with Sprint and me.
We'll take good care of you. You won't
have to lift a feather."

Flap's beak fell open. Three days?
That was much too long to stay here.

They had to find their way back home!

But the girls were chattering away excitedly.

"Or you could stay with Flick and me!" Felicity invited. "Living in a fox den is the best!"

Bree hopped up and down. "Twist and I have the best kitchen in Wonderwood. We'd love to cook for you!"

"Oooh!" Sage chimed in. "Stay with Caper and me! It's the most fun house in Wonderwood. Just sayin'."

Patter felt overwhelmed. The girls were all so kind and caring. "We peacocks are proud but right now we sure could use a helping hand …"

"Oohtaw!" Flick laid her furry paw on Patter's shoulder.

Patter laughed happily. "Or paw!"

Flap's tail feathers were drooping. He was unhappy. Patter pulled him aside to talk. "After what we've been through, I'd say we deserve to have some fun, don't you?"

Flap scratched his feet in the dirt. "Mmmmm…" he murmured uncertainly. He wouldn't look at Patter.

"It's only for a few days and we both love a good party, right?"

Flap sighed. "Mmhm," he agreed reluctantly. He really did want to make Patter happy. He wanted to be a good friend. He really did.

"Great!" said Patter. She turned to the girls. "We'd love to celebrate the Big Bloom with all of you!"

"Super!" Felicity clapped her hands. "We can figure out later which house you'll be staying at. Come on! Follow us!"

"Where are we going?" asked Patter, hurrying to catch up.

"Into town!" Bree explained. "We have to get all the supplies to start decorating the gazebo and all of our houses!" She took Patter's hand in hers and hopped away with her.

"Whoa!" Patter gasped. Her wings spread and her feet lifted into the air for a moment.

Flap watched her disappear. Was she going to forget all about him now that she had made new friends? He hoped not, but it sure looked like it.

CHAPTER SIX

SHOPPING SPREE

The village of Wonderwood was adorable. Tiny cottages surrounded a village square filled with flowers. There were cute cafés and beautiful boutiques. An ice cream truck was parked near a pretty gazebo.

Patter was impressed. "Wow! You said the town was cute, Bree, but you didn't say it was beautiful."

"Well, nobody likes a bunny bragger," Bree explained.

"Look, Flap! A gazebo!" Patter pointed. "And all the little shops and cafés and flowers. It's like an illustration from one of your favourite storybooks."

Flap's eyes were wide as he looked around. But he didn't say a word.

"C'mon, guys," said Felicity. "No time to waste. We've got some serious shopping to do!" She hurried towards the town's shop and everyone followed her inside.

"Well, hi, everyone!" called out

Bren as they entered. Her brown bear ears twitched happily. "What can I do for you today?"

"We're shopping for—" Bree began.

"The Big Bloom!" shouted everyone else in unison.

"Figured as much," said Bren. "Seems like everyone in town has come in today. Happy shopping!"

Felicity pulled Patter and Flap forwards. "We have some out-of-forest guests. This is Patter and her bestie, Flap," she said by way of introduction.

"Welcome to Wonderwood, you two," Bren said.

"Haroomph!" welcomed a gruff voice beside her. It was Bren's bear bestie, Snore, a sweet, bumbly fellow who worked behind the counter with her.

"This your first Big Bloom celebration?" asked Bren.

"Yes, it is," Patter answered politely. "We don't celebrate the Big Bloom in Junglewood."

Bren smiled kindly. "Well, with those fancy feathers, you'll certainly brighten up the celebration!"

Bree was getting the ingredients to bake a cake. Danessa was looking for a new flower vase and Felicity was checking out the fabrics and paints. Sage put boxes of decorative lights into her shopping basket. When they were all finished, Bren checked them out.

"Party food, party decorations, more party food, fabric, party food, lights... and more party food!" Bren laughed.

"That should do it," said Felicity.

Bren smiled. "Oh, and Patter, here's some complimentary honey for you and Flap. Welcome to Wonderwood." A cluster of bees flew over, holding a small jar in their fuzzy arms. Patter took the jar from them, amazed.

"Thanks so much!" she said to them. "That's very nice of you. Isn't it, Flap?"

Flap tried to smile but the corners of his beak barely turned up. Everyone else waved to Bren as they left the shop.

"Bye!" called Felicity.

"See you next time!" added Bree.

"Thank you!" Patter said.

Only when they were outside did Patter turn to Felicity. She looked at the little jar in her hands, confused. "What's honey?" she asked.

CHAPTER SEVEN

A PEACOCK POUTS

The girls stopped at the gazebo and put down their shopping bags. "Why don't we lighten our load a bit?" Felicity suggested.

A flock of robins flew over, picked up the shopping bags by their handles and flew off with them.

"Thank you very much!" Felicity

called after the birds.

Everyone in Wonderwood was so kind and helpful, thought Patter.

Sage stepped up on the platform. "Our besties will be performing a dance tonight." She turned to the animals, who were all crowded together. "How about a preview for our new friends?"

Twist thumped her paws. Caper swished her tail. Flick flicked her ears and Sprint tapped his hooves. They didn't have to be asked twice!

The girls sat down in front of the stage. Patter wrapped an arm around Flap and he snuggled close.

Onstage, the animals got into a line, each one holding on to the tail of the bestie in front of them. Twist thumped her paws again to start the rhythm.

The animals tapped the stage floor twice with their right paws. Then they tapped the floor twice with their left paws. They hopped forwards and they hopped backwards. Twist was leading.

Flap was having a hard time paying attention to the show. He was missing home too much. He used the tip of a feather to draw a picture of his home in Junglewood in the dirt. But no one noticed how sad he was, not even Patter. She was concentrating on the performance.

The animals still needed more rehearsals. They were having trouble staying in time. The skunk bumped into the deer and the deer stepped on the fox's tail. The bunny hopped too high and tumbled over.

Flomp!

Bloop!

Whomp!

Twist got up and began dancing on her own, thumping and hopping.

Bree shook her head. "It's called the Bunny Bounce! And you'll never guess who came up with the idea."

Onstage, Twist wiggled her ears, proud to be acknowledged.

"Good job, Twist," called Felicity.

"I love it!" said Sage.

Finally Danessa noticed that Flap wasn't paying any attention to the dance. "He looks sad," she said to Patter. "Is there anything I can do to help?"

Patter bit her lip uncertainly. "I don't think so. He hasn't said much since the storm."

"Sage, maybe you can cheer him up," Danessa suggested. "You're good at that."

Sage scampered over to where Flap was drawing in the dirt. "Hey!" she said cheerfully. "Wanna see a walrus?" She flipped her ponytail in front of her face and held it under her nose so it looked like a big, bushy walrus mustache.

But Flap just went back to staring at the dirt.

"OK," sighed Sage. "How about I make a funny sound?" She put one hand under her arm and flapped her elbow, making squeaky, farty noises. Bree giggled. Patter smiled. But Flap didn't even look up.

Sage threw up her hands. "Well, I tried. See you later." She got on to her feet and immediately pretended to trip. She glanced at Flap. Was he cracking a smile? Sage thought she might have glimpsed one. Still, she needed a better reaction than that.

"Hmmm," Sage said. "This stuff usually has 'em rolling in the aisles."

"Maybe he'll feel better once he's had a good night's sleep," Danessa suggested.

"Right," agreed Felicity. "So let's decide where our new friends will stay until the Big Bloom."

"We all want them to stay with us, so what do we do?" asked Sage.

Bree looked thoughtful. "Ladybirds!" she announced.

Danessa scratched

her antlers. "You want them to stay with ladybirds?"

"No! We use the Ladybird Decider. It's my latest invention," Bree laughed. She picked a geranium blossom. It was covered in ladybirds. "Ladybirds love geraniums and they also happen to like helping Enchantimals make decisions. It's very scientific."

She told all the girls to hold out their hands, palms up. When they did, the ladybirds flew from the geranium petals and landed on the girls. The besties scampered off the stage to watch what was happening.

"Now, count the spots on the ladybirds," instructed Bree. "Whoever has the most spots wins!"

"Three," announced Bree.

"Six!" Felicity exclaimed.

Danessa hung her head. She only had four.

Sage was confused. "I lost count," she said. Ladybirds were crawling all over her fingers.

"I think you win!" said Bree.

"Yep, that's a lot of ladybirds!" Felicity noted, looking at all of them.

Sage was thrilled. "I just know you're going to love it at our house," she told Patter.

"I'm sure we will!" Patter replied.

But now Bree had an even better idea. "Why don't we all take turns? Patter can come to our house bright and early tomorrow morning for breakfast."

"Then stay at our den tomorrow night!" Felicity exclaimed.

"And come to our house the next afternoon!" Danessa was excited. She was so looking forward to having the peacocks as guests.

Flap's tail feathers were twitching. He was feeling very nervous about all this moving around. When were he and Patter going to go home?

"All of that sounds lovely!" said Patter to her new friends. If only she noticed how upset Flap was becoming. But she didn't.

The girls began to go and get ready for the Big Bloom while the besties stayed behind to practise their dance routine. They invited Flap to join them.

Flap didn't know what to do. He didn't want to be rude but he did want to stay close to Patter.

"That's a great idea!" Patter said to the besties. "Flap loves to dance."

Caper grabbed Flap's wing and pulled him on to the stage.

Sage grinned. "Perfect. Flap will practise with these guys while we go ahead. Flap, Caper… see you later back at the house!"

Flap watched Patter disappear around a turn in the road. He hadn't felt this unhappy since their house had been destroyed. Now he felt sad and alone. Patter had left him with strangers. What was he going to do?

CHAPTER EIGHT

SILLY SAGE

Patter was feeling a little shy herself.
She chattered nervously with the girls.
"Off we go! This is so exciting. I love
parties. Love love love them! Dressing
up in fancy clothes. Wearing jewellery.
The Big Bloom! Catchy! Oh, I said that
before didn't I? Guess I'm a little nervous.
We've never been anywhere except

Junglewood. Flap and I had the most splendid house! Now it's gone. Gone gone gone. Blown away. Oh dear."

To calm herself, Patter began singing, or rather, squawking. "La-la-la-la-la!" It clearly made her feel better, so Sage tried not to cover her ears. After all, the other girls put up with her perfume. "Ah, much better," Patter said when she was done.

"Whatever works for you," replied Sage. "Here we are." They had reached the house where she lived with Caper. "Say, do you like funny jokes?"

"Of course," Patter answered.

"Too bad. All of mine stink." She waited a moment for Patter to get it. She giggled as Patter began to laugh. "A little skunk humour there! There's more where that came from."

Sage opened the door to her cottage. "Behold the fun-time factory," she announced.

The entire room was decorated in the prettiest shades of purple with some hints of pink. There was a pink bedspread, purple curtains and a pink rug. On the walls, which were painted lavender, were posters of all of Sage's favourite bands.

"It's pretty," Patter declared.

Sage picked up a bottle and began spritzing the room, releasing the powerful scent of jasmine and gardenia. "Nothing like a little perfume to really make the day special!" She sprayed Patter, too.

"Mmm!" said Patter, breathing in. "Smells lovely. Reminds me of the flowers at home."

"Great! Have another spritz. And

a seat!" exclaimed Sage.

Patter sat down on a chair – which let out a long squeaky, farty noise. Patter leaped up, embarrassed.

"Oops!" Sage giggled. "Forgot about that!" She reached under the chair pillow and pulled out a large whoopee cushion. "A classic! Sorry!"

"Don't apologise. It's hilarious." Patter smiled. "You're hilarious."

Patter had wandered over to the bookcase to look at Sage's photos. "Oh, is that you and Caper?" she asked, picking up one of the pictures. The moment she did, water sprayed out of a button and splashed her. "Agh!"

Sage hung her head, embarrassed. "Oh man. I should have warned you."

But Patter was laughing as she wiped

her face. "A photo that sprays water! I thought I'd seen everything."

"That photo's part of my prank collection." Sage handed Patter a tissue.

"You have a whole collection?" asked Patter.

"You betcha!"

Sage also owned a lot of musical instruments. She was in a band.

"Do you play all of those?" Patter asked.

"Yup," answered Sage. "Do you play?"

"No, but I'd love to learn."

Sage smiled at her new friend. "You are such a good sport," she told her. "We're gonna

have so much fun together. I just
know it."

"Me too!" agreed Patter. "I just hope
Flap's having as much fun as I am."

He wasn't.

CHAPTER NINE

NO FUN FOR FLAP

The besties were doing their best to include Flap but it wasn't easy.

"Flap, Flap," said Twist to get the peacock's attention. The bunny jumped into the air, then jumped a little higher and she soared up, up, up. She landed right next to Flap, startling him. He squawked. His tail feathers spread out in a fan of surprise.

Flick decided to take control of the rehearsal and told all the besties they were going to try the dance again from the beginning.

Everyone took their places. Caper wanted to help Flap relax, so she sprayed him with perfume. "Mmmmmm," the skunk purred happily.

Flap coughed and coughed. A fly flew into his open beak. Flap spat it out.

Sprint trotted over. He was worried about Flap. He took Flap gently by the wing and led him to the front of the line. Maybe that would make him feel more included.

"Towee!" chirped Flick. What a good idea!

Only it wasn't. The besties began their

bunny-hop dance but every time Sprint hopped forward, the deer accidentally poked Flap with his antlers.

"Oo-fa!" He whinnied an apology. "Oo-fa! Oops! Oo-fa, da!"

Flap was miserable. He didn't want to dance and he didn't want to make new friends and he certainly didn't want to be poked by a deer, even if it was an accident. He wanted to go home to Junglewood.

But it was different for Patter. She was really enjoying playing music with Sage. She was having so much fun that she found herself thinking less and less about finding a way to return to their home.

While Sage strummed her guitar, Patter let loose on the drums. She didn't even notice when Caper and Flap entered the cottage. Flap winced at the racket the girls were making.

Sage was thrilled to see the besties. "Caper! Flap! You're just in time! Join the band!"

Caper grabbed two drumsticks in her paws and began tapping out a rhythm on every surface she could hit – bedposts, hanging plants and even the whoopee cushion. *Tap! Tap! Bang! Bang!*

Flap was exhausted. He hoped their performance would end soon. But Sage had another instrument she wanted to try out – an accordion!

"I'm still learning," Sage yelled over the noise. "But I think I'm getting the hang of it." She pressed her fingers down hard on the buttons for one last wailing note. "Great stuff, right?"

But Flap couldn't take it any more. He hid under the bed.

CHAPTER TEN

CARROT CHAOS

The next morning, Patter and Flap headed over to the bunny cottage for breakfast. Bree and Twist had an enormous garden in the front of their house filled with carrots, cabbage, lettuce, broccoli and all kinds of wonderful vegetables.

Bree took Patter and Flap inside to show them her favourite room – the kitchen! It was filled with Bree's time-saving inventions, from turning wheels to buzzing conveyor belts. Twist was ready to cook up a feast.

"Let's start with some breakfast," Bree suggested.

Twist hopped on to a button and a sandwich-making machine began whirring. Two mechanical hands picked up slices of bread, slathered them with mayonnaise and lined them with lettuce.

"Hope you like lettuce sandwiches," said Bree.

"We've never had them before," Patter admitted. "We eat mostly seeds and berries."

"Well, then, you're in for a real treat!"

exclaimed Bree.

Patter took a delicate nibble. "Mmmm. Tasty," she said politely.

Flap sniffed the sandwich, scrunched up his face and turned away.

Twist was watching Flap, her nose and whiskers twitching. She chirped and squeaked, asking Flap if he was going to finish the sandwich.

Flap slid it across the table to the bunny. He was not even going to try it. He'd rather go hungry.

Patter had noticed the family photos covering Bree's refrigerator. There were old bunnies and young bunnies, huge rabbits and little cottontails. "Are those Twist's relatives?" asked Patter.

"Yup!" answered Bree. "She's got a pretty big family." She pointed over to a cabinet where there were dozens more photos of bunnies.

"Wow!" Patter exclaimed.

Twist hopped over and began telling the guests who everyone was. "Fluffy! Fluff-Fluff! Fluffers! Fliff Flaff!"

Patter picked up one of the photos to look at it more carefully – and got sprayed by a jet of water! It was another prank picture frame.

"Oops!" apologised Bree. "Sage gave us that one!"

Patter grinned. "I should have guessed."

"Let's get baking!" Bree suggested.

Patter was excited. "What are we going to make?"

"As if there's a choice?" Bree giggled. "Carrot cakes, of course. Moist.

Delicious. And orange!"

Twist looked hungrily at all the carrots laid out on the counter. Carrots were the best!

Patter admitted that she had never made a cake before.

"It's easy-peasy carrot-squeezy. Especially with my brand-new carrot cake machine that I just invented. You'll be the first to see it in action." Bree held up a bunch of carrots. "Guess where these came from?"

"The refrigerator?" answered Patter uncertainly.

Bree laughed. "Before that! Our very own vegetable garden!"

"We don't have carrots in the jungle," explained

Patter. "Do we, Flap?"

Flap shook his head. Twist couldn't believe it. She was shocked. How could you live without carrots?

Bree handed Flap a single carrot. "Here ya go. I'll demonstrate how my machine works, then you can use it yourself. You just put the carrot right in here."

Flap slid the carrot into a funnel at the top of the contraption.

"Good, Flap!" said Bree. "Now you can press this button."

The peacock pressed the button with his claw and the machine began humming. Scissors sliced off the top of the carrot and a set of blades juiced the greens.

"We can drink that later. I call it

carrot-top smoothie," Bree told her
guests.

Patter tried to pretend that sounded
delicious to her. "Mmmmm," she said.

Grated carrot was whizzing through
the machine into a large mixing bowl.

"Excellent work," Bree exclaimed.
"I think you're ready to do all the rest
of the carrots while Twist and I make
the frosting."

"Woo-hoo!" shouted Twist, excited.

Patter gulped, looking at the huge
pile of carrots on the counter. "All
of them?"

"Yep!" answered Bree happily.
"All of them."

Flap and Patter exchanged worried
glances. Patter began dropping all the
carrots into the funnel while Flap pressed

the start button. But they didn't have
the right rhythm and soon the carrots
were jamming in the machine and pieces
of grated carrot were flying all over the
kitchen!

"Ikes!" squeaked Twist.

"Did you put all of the carrots in at
once?" asked Bree.

"Yep, just like you said," Patter
answered.

"Oh no!" squealed Bree. "I didn't
mean all at once!"

"You didn't?" Patter cried. "Oops!"

Carrots were still flying through the
air and Twist was catching as many
as she could in her teeth. They were
delicious!

But the carrots were hitting Flap,
who covered his head with his wings.

Patter tried to turn off the machine, but when she pressed the button, nothing happened. Now water was shooting out of it. The greens were flying right up like an erupting volcano of smoothie!

"Yikes!" exclaimed Bree.

"Aaaaaaah!" Twist grabbed a bin lid and began using it as a shield.

"How do you stop this thing?" Patter asked Bree desperately.

Bree shrugged, embarrassed. "Well...you see..." she stammered. "The thing is...I didn't quite get around to creating a stop button."

But Twist was thinking. The bunny scurried low to the ground across the kitchen floor. She pulled the plug from the socket! Everything stopped. Silence.

"Note to self," said Bree, taking out

a notebook and jotting something down,
"stop buttons are very important!"

CHAPTER ELEVEN

A FOXY FIASCO

Later that day, Patter and Flap headed over to the fox den to help Felicity and Flick get ready for the Big Bloom. They knocked on the door.

Felicity answered it. "There you are!" she said. "Right on time. We just finished cleaning."

The den was built into the side of

a hill and mostly underground. There were travel posters on the walls of all the places that Felicity had visited – and rare gems she'd collected as souvenirs on the bookshelves. There were lots of books in the small room, but it was very cosy and very clean.

"Look, Flap!" Patter pointed at the bookshelves. "He loves to read," she explained to Felicity.

"They're all categorised by subject, in alphabetical order by author," Felicity told her guests proudly. "And later, after we all wash our hands, we can read them."

Flap was looking at a map on the wall. It showed all of Everwilde. He found Junglewood. Now he could see just how far away their home really was.

"It's even further than we thought," noted Patter.

"All the more reason to stick around, right?" said Felicity cheerfully. She went over to the windows and drew the curtains. Foxes like the darkness. "There! That's cosier. Now for some fun!"

Felicity unrolled a big roll of fabric on the floor in order to, she explained, make bunting.

"What's that?" Patter asked.

"Festive fabric to decorate the gazebo and the stage," said Felicity. "We'll use the rest to decorate our windows. I've cut it into strips and picked out some paint."

Flick was balancing a paint can on her head and she had a brush in her mouth.

Flap was shivering. The den was cold

and dark, and he couldn't stop looking at the map. How would they ever get back to Junglewood?

Felicity opened up the can of paint and handed paintbrushes to Patter and Flap. "We're painting these strips green," she explained. " 'Cause that's the colour of spring!"

Flap went to help, but as he did, his long tail feathers brushed across a table and sent Felicity's sparkly gem collection tumbling to the floor.

"Ooof!" squawked Flap, trying to catch the gems.

Patter apologised for her bestie. "I'm so sorry! Flap's tail feathers…"

Felicity carefully put her precious stones back in place. "That's OK," she said, taking a big breath. "None of my gems got broken." But she did suggest that Flap stand over by the door, where he wouldn't get in the way. Unfortunately, as the peacock strutted across the den, his tail feathers swept a whole row of books on to the floor!

Flick dived to catch them as they fell. "Incoming!" she shouted.

"Oh dear," Patter laughed nervously. "That's the thing about tail feathers. They have a mind of their own!"

Felicity took another deep breath. "Don't worry. They're just books. Brand. New. Books." She began putting them on the shelf. "Let's see. I believe this one goes under 'small burrowing mammals' in the D section ..."

"It's kind of dark in here," Patter chattered, trying to excuse her bestie.

"I guess Flap didn't see them."

The den was tiny, that was the problem. Flap turned to study the map on the wall and bumped into the open can of paint. It spilled.

Patter panicked. "We're so sorry!"

Felicity rushed over and slid on the slippery floor, careening into Flap, who fell on to Patter. *Sploosh! Splash! Splat!* What a mess!

"I'm so sorry," Patter kept saying over and over again. "We'll try to be more careful." But the words were barely out of her mouth when she stumbled and kicked another open can of paint. It flipped into the air and landed with a splat right on Felicity's head.

Felicity laughed, trying to be positive. "Who says foxes have to be red?" she joked, wiping green paint off her face.

Patter was overwhelmed and when she was overwhelmed, she always began singing. If you could call it that.

"La-la-la-laa," she sang under her breath, trying to calm herself down.

"Let's forget about the bunting," Felicity suggested. "You two can turn in early and get a good night's sleep. I'm just going to tidy up…for a few hours."

CHAPTER TWELVE
DANESSA'S DISASTER

Danessa welcomed the peacocks to her cabin the next morning. Deep in the woods, the cosy cabin was almost entirely hidden by fragrant berry bushes.

"Welcome, you two," Danessa said in her calm, quiet voice. "How was your night at Felicity's?"

"Slippery," Patter answered truthfully.

"And Flap loved being surrounded by so many books."

Flap was confused. Did Patter really think he'd had a good time?

Danessa welcomed them both into her home. Flowering plants hung from the windows. There were big beanbag chairs and colourful rag rugs. There were vases filled with wildflowers. It was almost like being outside.

Danessa and Sprint hovered close to their guests. They wanted to take very good care of them.

"I'm so glad you could spend some time with us," said Danessa. "I hope you're having a good time in Wonderwood."

Patter nodded. "Thank you. You and your friends have all been so kind and generous to us."

"Well, that's what we do!" Danessa smiled at her. "Everyone is welcome in Wonderwood. Enchantimals come for a visit and never leave. Hey, you two could stay for ever, too!"

Flap gasped and stared at Patter. She couldn't be thinking of staying for ever. Could she? For ever was an awfully long time.

"It's definitely worth thinking about," responded Patter. "Your place is so nice and cosy."

Danessa gestured around the room. "You're welcome to my bed, my favourite chair, my food, whatever you need … anything at all!" She blinked her long eyelashes, waiting for her guests to say something. "You look hungry. Do you

want a snack? Something to drink? A
pillow? A nap?"

Patter shrugged. "We're good.
Really."

"Great!" said Danessa, relieved.
Sprint cantered out of the room to get
something. "Because we have some work
to do. Fun work! Big Bloom work. You're
so lucky you arrived in our forest at the
most magical time of the year."

"I know," agreed Patter. "I can hardly
wait until tonight. We peacocks love a
good party."

"We're in charge of making the flower
centrepieces!" Danessa continued. "And
as you can see, we love flowers! I love
to water them, smell them and talk to
them." She bent down and whispered
quietly to one of her plants.

Sprint strolled back into the room carrying a bunch of baskets in his mouth. They were brimming with pretty daisies and big rhododendron blossoms.

"Ooh!" exclaimed Patter. "They're gorgeous. We've never seen these before. We have different flowers in our jungle. Don't we, Flap?"

Flap nodded.

Danessa was beginning to arrange the flowers. "All we have to do," she told the others, "is take two daisies from this basket and two rhododendrons from this basket and place them in pretty vases."

"Sounds easy," said Patter.

"It is easy," Danessa agreed.

Patter was choosing her flowers and repeating the directions to herself. "Two daisies and two...rho-do-den-drons.

Pretty, right, Flap?"

"Achoo!" Flap opened his beak and sneezed loudly.

"Achoo!" Patter echoed his sneeze.

"Achoo!" They both sneezed together.

"Bless you!" said Danessa and Sprint together. "Are you OK?"

"Yes, just fine—" Patter began before sneezing again.

"Achoo!" Patter and Flap sneezed together.

Danessa was worried. "We'll get you some tissues, but it looks like you might be allergic to the flowers!"

"ACHOO!"

Patter fell back against the wall after her giant sneeze and crashed into a painting. "I'm OK." She sniffled.

Sprint handed her a tissue.

Danessa picked up the broken frame of the painting. "No biggie. I never liked it anyway."

Patter and Flap wiped their noses but it was no use. They couldn't stop sneezing. "Achoo! Achoo! ACHOO!"

"These tissues smell like flowers, too!" Patter said.

"They're rose-scented," Danessa realised. "Oh, that's not good. Sorry! Sprint!"

Sprint hurled the tissue box into the next room. But there were flowers everywhere. There was no way to get away from them – except to leave.

"We hate to sneeze and run," said Patter. "Achoo! But we've gotta get outta here now!"

Patter and Flap raced for the door

and bolted out of the cabin.

"Please come back later!" Danessa called after them. "I'll get the air purifier!"

CHAPTER THIRTEEN
DISAPPEARING ACT

Patter and Flap flew into the woods, far from Danessa's cabin and the smell of flowers. They sat down on a thick patch of green moss.

"Well," said Patter, taking a deep breath. "That was an experience. Finally, some fresh air. I don't know how many times we sneezed in there. I lost count after, like, a zillion."

Flap nodded and rubbed his beak.

"Oh, your poor little beak," said Patter. "It's as red as a hibiscus flower after a long jungle rain!"

Patter smoothed Flap's ruffled tail feathers. "Things will get better, Flap," she said reassuringly. "I'm sure of it. Everyone's so nice in Wonderwood and the Big Bloom sounds like it's going to be even more fun than Junglepalooza!"

Flap frowned. He didn't believe her.

Patter bit her lip thoughtfully. "How about what Danessa said about staying here permanently? I mean, we have nowhere to go and it's really great here, don't you think?"

Flap dropped his head. He wouldn't meet her eyes. He sneezed. Patter didn't understand how upset he was.

"C'mon, Flap," she said to her bestie. "Things aren't so bad. We should think about it." And then she had a good idea. "Over ice cream!"

She took Flap by the wing and led him to the village. She remembered seeing an ice cream truck there when they'd first arrived. This was clearly the perfect moment to check it out. Flap needed some cheering up.

The peacock-girl and her bestie fluttered back toward the village square. The ice cream truck was still parked near the gazebo.

"Look, there it is!" exclaimed Patter.

"Hi there!" said the owner, whose name was Preena. Her black-and-white hair matched the colouring of her penguin bestie. "Look at you with your pretty feathers. What can I get for you today?"

Patter studied the menu. "Well, let's see..."

"Our special flavour of the day is carrot cake."

"Anything but that," Patter said hurriedly. They'd had enough carrots recently. "Surprise us!"

"You got it," said Preena, who got to work scooping with her bestie Jayla. Preena and Jayla handed cones to Patter and Flap.

Their faces lit up when they tasted them. Delicious!

Flap sighed happily. He breathed a long sigh of relief. The taste of home.

"We love raspberries," Patter

explained. "Back in Junglewood, where we're from, Flap and I would go raspberry picking all the time!" She took another taste. "Do I detect mustard seeds? They're our favourite!"

"Never met a bird who could resist them!" Preena laughed.

Flap devoured his cone, burped and giggled. He smiled for the first time in days.

Patter was chattering away with Preena and Jayla. "Excuse me, but you're not from the forest, are you?" she asked.

"We're originally from Frozenwood," explained Preena. "But a while back, we thought it would be fun to share our ice cream with the rest of the land. So we packed up the truck for a little adventure."

"That's quite a change," Patter noted. "Weren't you scared?"

"At first," Preena admitted. "But then we started having so much fun meeting other Enchantimals and besties. I guess the 'scared' just melted away. Everyone was so friendly and welcoming, we decided to stay."

"We're actually thinking of staying here ourselves!" Patter told her.

Flap's beak fell open. Patter sounded serious!

"You should!" Preena told Patter.

"You don't miss your home?" Patter asked her.

"I'll always love Frozenwood, but as long as

I have my truck and my bestie, I always feel like I'm at home," Preena replied.

"Ya too!" added Jayla.

"That's really cool," said Patter. "What do you think, Flap? Flap?"

The peacock had disappeared.

"Flap? Flap? Flap!" Patter called for him, but she didn't see him anywhere. "Where did you go?"

"He must be close. Besties never wander far," Preena said reassuringly.

But Patter was worried. "I know, but I don't see him anywhere. Flap? Are you playing hide-and-seek or something? Because now's not the time, OK? FLAP! WHERE ARE YOU?"

Patter raced back towards the forest. Maybe he had returned to one of their new friends' cottages. Oh, she had to find him. He was her bestie. She couldn't lose him!

"We'll keep a lookout for him!" called Preena.

"Flap! Flap!" called Patter.

Where was he?

CHAPTER FOURTEEN

A NEW GAME OF HIDE-AND-SEEK

Patter rushed over to Sage's house. "Flap is lost!" she told the skunks breathlessly.

"Don't worry," said Sage. "We'll find him. We skunks have a really strong sense of smell. Don't we, Caper?"

Caper twitched her nose in agreement.

"Remind me," Sage said. "What does Flap smell like?"

Patter sniffed her own hands. Flap smelled like a peacock, like her. Only now that smell was hidden by the scents of perfume, carrot cake, paint and flowers. Patter tried to describe all those odours to Sage.

"Sounds like you guys have been pretty busy!" said Sage. She suggested they head over to Bree's to see if the bunnies knew anything.

"Flap is gone!" Patter announced as they approached. The bunnies were in the garden pulling up carrots. "We got some ice cream and then he just vanished!"

"We'll help you find him," Bree promised. "With all the carrots we eat, if

anyone can spot him, we can. C'mon!"
They all headed to Danessa's home.

"Arrot ake tream?" Twist asked
Patter, wondering if she'd gotten the
carrot cake ice cream.

But before Patter could answer, they
had arrived at Danessa's. All talking
at once, they told the deer-girl about the
missing peacock.

"Flap is missing?" Danessa was very
concerned.

"Yes!" cried Patter. "I have no idea
where he could be!"

"Oh no, you must be so worried."
Danessa patted her shoulder.

"I am," Patter sighed. "We need to
find him."

"C'mon!" Danessa told everyone.
"Felicity will know what to do."

By the time they arrived at the fox den, Felicity was already on the case. She had a map in her hand.

"I'm on it! Crickets, sound the alert," she announced.

A deafening chirping filled the forest. Preena and Jayla put down their ice cream scoops. Bren and Snore from the town shop stepped outside to see what was happening. This was an emergency!

Felicity held up her hand and a large trumpet flower floated down on to her open palm. She spoke through the flower like a megaphone. "Attention, all Enchantimals in Wonderwood Village! We have a lost bestie who answers to the name of Flap. If you find him, please bring him to the gazebo! Thank you! Oh, and did I mention? Flap's a peacock! And ... he's adorable!"

"What do we do now?" Bree asked.

Felicity was thinking. "Our best chance to find Flap is if we split up. Patter, Bree and Twist can cover the forest. The skunks and the deer can take the meadow. Flick and I will head to the Babbling Brook. She might be able to shed some light on where Flap could be."

Danessa took Patter's hand in hers. "Don't worry, Patter. We'll find Flap." She turned to all the girls. "Group hug, everyone?"

Everyone crowded around to give Patter a warm embrace.

Sage laughed. "Those feathers sure do

tickle!"

Patter was touched by how thoughtful and kind her new friends were. "Thanks, you guys."

"Good luck, everyone!" said Felicity. It was time for them to split up. They had to find Flap!

Felicity and Flick searched the village, hurrying from one shop to another. Their bushy red tails flicked back and forth urgently. They got Bren and Snore to put a 'Missing Peacock' sign up on the door.

The skunks and the deer searched the meadow filled with flowers. They kept stopping to listen for sneezes, but they didn't hear anything. The penguins drove their ice cream truck up and down the village lanes.

Patter and the bunnies looked behind every tree in the forest. Bree and Twist hopped as high as they could so they could see into the distance. Patter flew from branch to branch.

Caper froze in the middle of the meadow. "La-da," she told the others.

"What do you mean 'stop'?" Sage asked her bestie. "Do you see Flap?"

"No," whispered Sprint. "Hee-tah."

Everybody tried to be absolutely still to hear what Sprint was listening to. There it was! A faint chirping sound.

What could it be? Was it Flap?

CHAPTER FIFTEEN

A ROBIN RESCUE

A small robin lay in the grass, chirping weakly.

"It's hurt," gasped Sage.

"Hurt?" Danessa said worriedly. "What do you mean?"

The robin tried to flap its wing but could only tremble.

"Its wing is sprained," Sage realised.

"It's going to need a splint," said Danessa.

"We don't have time for that." Sage sighed. "We need to find Flap before it gets dark." The last thing they needed was two hurt birds.

But Danessa had a plan. "I guess it's time for nature to work its magic!" she announced.

Caper and Sprint grinned.

"First we need a soft bed for the bird." Danessa bent over towards the bird and held it while Sprint used his antlers to create a furrow in the grass. Suddenly, a bed of thornless roses began to bloom, creating a soft and fragrant bed.

"Whoa!" Sage exclaimed. "Someone's been practising his enchantments!"

Danessa gently placed the robin in

the bed of roses and stroked its feathered head. "That's it," she murmured. "Just relax. Everything's going to be all right."

Sage's brow furrowed. "Too bad Patter's not here. She could sing to it to calm it down."

Danessa, Caper and Sprint stared at her, stunned. Hadn't she heard Patter's off-key warbling?

"Seriously?" asked Danessa.

"OK," agreed Sage. "Maybe not. Do your thing, Sprint."

This time when Sprint used his antlers to scrape a line in the grass, healing herbs sprang up.

Sage nodded, pleased. "Another totally excellent enchantment."

Danessa picked the herbs carefully, crushed them with her fingers and sprinkled them on the robin's wing. A few moments later, the bird's feathers began to flutter.

"Look! It's working!" Sage said.

The robin began flapping its wings. It stood up on its feet and began chirping happily. It felt all better! Then the robin flew into the air and disappeared. A red feather floated down and landed between Sprint's antlers.

"A beautiful feather for good luck," said Danessa. Danessa pointed high up to a nearby tree where the robin had settled into a nest. "There's its home."

"Imagine being able to fly," said Sage.

"Birds are such special animals," Danessa noted. "They're so different from us mammals."

Her eyes widened as she realised what she had said. She'd been thinking like a mammal looking for Flap. But he was a bird. "New plan," Danessa announced. "No more searching in the meadow."

The others wanted to know why. But there was no time to explain.

"C'mon, we have to hurry!" Danessa told them, already beginning to race in a different direction. She hoped they weren't too late.

Sage waved goodbye to the robin. "Take care, little friend!"

CHAPTER SIXTEEN

A GLIMPSE INTO THE PAST

F elicity and Flick were looking for Flap near the Babbling Brook. But Felicity felt they needed some extra help and a little luck. "Can you find us a four-leaf clover?" she asked her bestie.

The fox set to work immediately, using her paws to look through the grass.

carried him away.

"Poor Flap!" said both Felicity and Flick.

They watched as Patter raced after her bestie. The wind was tossing the poor peacock this way and that way. He landed in the rushing waters of the Babbling Brook.

"Oh no!" Felicity gasped.

Flap grabbed a floating log but the current was carrying him away. Patter dived into the brook after him but there was no way for them to swim to shore. The waters were too wild. They were swept away in the rapids. Their house disappeared behind them. Patter and Flap held on tightly to the log. There was nothing else they could do. Finally, at last, when the brook reached Wonderwood, it began to widen and calm down. Patter and Flap were able to swim to shore. They were exhausted.

Felicity shook her head. "How awful," she said to Flick. "Did you see the look on Flap's face as he floated far away from his home?"

Flick nodded. It was so sad!

Felicity expressed her gratitude to the brook for showing them what had happened to their new friends. "Thank you, Babbling Brook," she said. "Your visions have given me an idea."

Flick cocked her head, curious.

But there was no time to lose. "I think I know where Flap might be!" announced

Felicity, already hurrying off.

Flick was confused, but she scampered after her. They had to find the lost bestie!

CHAPTER SEVENTEEN
INTO THE WOODS

Bree and Twist had gone back with Patter to the place where everyone had first met in the forest. Maybe Flap had returned to the leaf pile where he had been found during hide-and-seek.

Patter was worried. "Flap! Where are you? Flap!"

"Flap!" called Twist.

Bree noticed her bunny bestie was studying the ground and realised what she was doing. "That's right," she complimented her. "Maybe you'll find one of his feathers."

Patter burst into tears. "Ooh, his feathers," she cried. "His beautiful feathers. If anything's happened to Flap, I'll never forgive myself."

"Don't say that, Patter," Bree said. "It's not your fault."

But Patter felt like it was. "I should've listened to him more. I shouldn't have ignored his feelings. I mean, what if we never ever find him? What if we search and search every single inch of Everwilde and he still doesn't show up? I can't imagine what I'd do!"

Patter was upset, and when she was

upset, she squawked.

Bree and Twist tried to keep from covering their ears. But they couldn't. The noise was just too horrible.

"La-la-la-la-la-la-la!" Patter was singing at the top of her lungs. "La-la-la-la-la!"

Tears fell from her eyes. "I should have paid attention to how sad he looked. I'd give anything in the world to see Flap's smile again."

Bree thumped her on the back, trying to comfort her. "He smiles?" she asked.

Patter nodded. "All the time. Just not since we've come to Wonderwood." She paused, blinking. She wiped away her tears. That wasn't entirely true. "Wait a minute. Raspberry and mustard seeds!"

Bree was confused. "Peacocks have

the strangest expressions!"

"Ya, ya," agreed Twist.

"No!" Patter laughed, suddenly happy. "The ice cream! Flap smiled when he ate the ice cream from the penguins! I think I know where he is!"

"At the ice cream truck?" asked Bree.

"No," said Patter, but there was no time for an explanation. "C'mon. Follow me."

Bree and Twist hopped as fast as they could to keep up with Patter as she headed deeper and deeper into the woods.

Meanwhile, Danessa was racing through another part of the forest with Sprint leaping close behind her. Sage and Caper

were having a hard time keeping up with the deer.

"Slow down!" Sage begged Danessa. "Where are you leading us?"

"To Flap, I hope!" Danessa called back over her shoulder.

"But how do you know where he is?" asked Sage.

"I can just feel it in my antlers," Danessa explained. "It's a deer thing."

Felicity and Flick were also racing through the woods.

"We're coming for you, Flap!" Felicity shouted into the trees.

Flick narrowed her eyes, determined to find the peacock.

The sun was sinking, the day was ending and the forest was becoming darker and darker. Would they ever find the peacock? This hide-and-seek game was no fun at all!

CHAPTER EIGHTEEN

COMING HOME

Flap fluttered from one branch to another. His feathers were drooping. He was tired but he was also determined. He was going home.

He passed the Babbling Brook and stopped for a drink. He was thirsty. The current carried a four-leaf clover past him and Flap watched it as it spun around and around. There in the water he could see all that had happened to him. He saw himself and Patter being swept away from their home. He saw their home flattened by the tree. He saw the wild winds of the storm. And he saw all the good times, too. He missed their garden and their swing and their veranda. Most of all, he missed Patter.

The water swirled and became darker. Flap saw Patter looking for him. He saw how upset she was. He saw all the other girls and their besties searching the forest to find out where he had gone. He was surprised. He didn't think anyone cared about him. How could he possibly go home to Junglewood without Patter? Home wouldn't be home without her.

Two butterflies danced across the

brook and Flap watched them. On the other bank he saw two bunnies playing together. In the trees, birds were tweeting to one another and cuddling close in their nests as the sun began to set. Maybe it wasn't so bad here after all. Maybe he didn't have to leave right away. Maybe he could stay a little while. He turned around and headed back towards the village of Wonderwood.

In another part of the forest, the different search teams were meeting up with one another.

"Hey, everyone!" Sage exclaimed. "Fancy meeting you here."

"Have you found Flap?" Patter

asked anxiously.

Felicity shook her head. "No, not yet. But I think he's very close!"

"Me too!" agreed Danessa.

"Me three!" Bree chimed in.

"Me four!" added Sage.

Patter looked from one girl to another. "I guess we all had the same idea. We all know where Flap is heading, right?"

"Junglewood!" shouted everyone at once.

"Home," corrected Patter.

Flick gasped. "Avalay!" she shouted, getting everyone's attention. She held up a peacock feather.

Sage sniffed it. She sniffed it

again. "Perfume," she announced, like a detective. "And carrot cake. And the lingering aroma of homesickness."

"You can smell homesickness?" asked Patter.

Sage shrugged. "It's a skunk thing."

"He must be really close," Felicity realised.

And he was. A shadow emerged through the trees. The shadow looked like a peacock. It was a peacock! It was Flap. Patter raced towards him and he flew towards her. They wrapped each other up in a big hug of arms and wings. They spun around in a circle and their feet lifted off the ground.

"Oh, Flap!" cried Patter. "I'm so glad we found you! You had me so worried! All of us!"

Everyone was thrilled. The bunnies wiggled their tails, the skunks did somersaults and Sprint took the robin's feather from his antlers and waved it around.

"Yay!"

"Yippee!"

"Hooray!"

"You were going home, weren't you?" Patter asked Flap.

Flap nodded.

But Patter had just realised something. She was confused. "But you were headed towards Wonderwood!"

Flap grinned. He told her that he had changed his mind.

"I don't understand," said Patter. "Why?"

Flap threw his wings around Patter

again. "Flap, Patter. Patter and Flap, Flatter and Plat," he gushed. She knew what he was saying to her. She always did. "Me and you. We belong together. Always."

Patter wiped tears from her eyes. Of course they did. She knew that. "As long as you and I are together, we'll always be home. No matter where we are."

"Because home is where your best friend is," said Danessa. She patted Sprint.

Still, there was something Patter had to say to Flap. "I'm so sorry," she apologised. "I guess I just got caught up with this exciting new place and I didn't think about your feelings. Will you ever forgive me?"

Flap let out a long happy chirp. Of

course he would.

"Awwww," everyone said.

Sage grinned. "Tickle hug!" She embraced the peacocks, and everybody wrapped their arms, their paws and their tails around one another and giggled happily.

"Thanks for your help, you guys," said Patter when they pulled apart.

Felicity took a deep breath. She'd been thinking about something. "So," she announced, "while you two may always be home, you still need a house!"

Patter and Flap looked at each other, confused.

But Felicity had a plan. An excellent plan. She led them all to the run-down cottage at the edge of the village. "OK," she admitted. "It's not exactly the most charming place in Wonderwood …"

A broken shingle clattered on to the porch. Patter and Flap looked uncertain.

But Felicity knew that teamwork could make anything happen.

"By the time we're done with it…" Felicity said.

"It will be your very own home," finished Danessa.

"Made especially for you and your needs," said Bree.

"A perfect home for our new friends," Danessa told them. "So, what do you say?"

"Will you stay with us?" asked Sage.

"Will you make Wonderwood your new home?" Felicity pleaded, smiling.

Patter turned to her bestie. "I'll do whatever Flap wants. We can go back to Junglewood if he likes and rebuild our house and return to our life there ..."

Flap rubbed his beak with his wing, thoughtful.

"Or is Wonderwood a place where you'll be happy?" Patter asked him. "A place you could call home?"

Flap opened his beak to speak, then shut it and waited. It was a big decision, after all. And what helped him make it were the smiling faces of the Enchantimals and their besties. They were all so nice and helpful. They really were.

"Chip, chip, chiree!" announced Flap. YES! A big smile spread across his face.

Patter was thrilled. "There you have it! We definitely, positively want to call Wonderwood our home!"

Everyone cheered – and the noise caused another part of the house to crumble.

"As far as this house goes, though, we're not so sure," joked Patter.

Everyone laughed.

They had a lot of work to do, but they were ready!

CHAPTER NINETEEN
THE BIG BLOOM

Felicity scampered to her roof. She used a trumpet flower to magnify her voice as she made an important announcement. "Attention, all Enchantimals and besties! Flap the peacock has been found!"

A roar of happiness spread through the village. Preena and Jayla rubbed their beaks together. Bren and Snore high-fived with their paws.

"We're inviting everyone to our party after we help build a home for two very special birds," continued Felicity. "We want to welcome our newest neighbours to Wonderwood Village. It'll be the biggest and bloomiest Big Bloom celebration of all time!"

But first they had some work to do. They had a house to repair. Everyone helped out. The robins carried tools in their beaks, the tortoises balanced paint cans on their backs and the penguins kept everyone happy with ice cream. They hammered and they sawed. They painted and they polished. The window frames were painted purple, there were green and yellow accents on the porch and the shutters were a vivid blue. The whole house began to look as beautiful as a peacock.

Bree planted berry bushes in the front garden and all it took was a little special care to have them blooming in an instant. Bree also made a weather vane and Patter flew up to the roof and attached it to one of the turrets. It was a peacock and it was just like the one from their house in Junglewood. It made Flap smile.

Sage painted the inside of the house a beautiful shade of lavender. Danessa brought in vases and filled them with leafy branches. She was careful to make sure there were no flowers anywhere that would make the peacocks sneeze. Felicity hung green-and-white curtains at the windows. Bree filled the kitchen with delicious food from her garden, making sure to include a boxful of raspberries and a jar of mustard seeds.

When the whole house was just about done, Danessa positioned a pile of pillows at the bottom of the stairs. It was time to slide down the banister! One after another the besties slid down and careened into the pillows, laughing. But there wasn't too much extra time for silliness. They had to celebrate the Big Bloom – and they were going to do it in Patter and Flap's front garden.

There were tables covered with carrot cakes. Pretty paper lanterns were strung from tree to tree. Sage was playing the guitar and a trio of crickets accompanied her.

Felicity approached an amazed Patter

and Flap. "So? What do you think?"

"No crazy kitchen!" Bree reminded them.

"No flowers to make you sneeze!" added Danessa.

"No loud music," promised Sage. "And no picture frames that spray water. OK, OK, maybe one."

"Nice and warm with plenty of room to flap your wings or perch on a rafter," Felicity pointed out.

Patter turned to Flap. His opinion was what mattered to her. "What do you think?" she asked him.

Flap was quiet. He looked at the garden. He looked at the house. Everyone was waiting. They could barely breathe.

Flap's blue eyes sparkled. "La-la-la-la-LOVE!" he announced.

Everyone cheered.

"Well, your home is now complete, but we have one last surprise for you," Felicity said. She whistled and a cloud of fireflies, their lights flashing in the darkness, formed a huge heart over the house.

Patter reached out and held Flap's wing. Together, they flew up to a perch above the porch. Patter addressed the crowd. "Flap and I would like to thank all of you from the bottom of our hearts for your thoughtfulness and, most of all, your unstoppable caring."

"What can we say?" Felicity laughed, delighted. "Caring is our everything!"

"We're proud as peacocks," Patter continued, "to call you our friends – no, not just friends – our family! You shared

yourselves with us and gave us a home,
and for that we're forever grateful. I'm
going to stop now, because if I continue,
I'll get even more nervous and I'll have
to sing. And we all know I have a terrible
voice!"

Flap spread his tail feathers and
opened his beak. He began to sing.

No one could believe what they were
hearing! The peacock was singing, and
his voice, unlike Patter's, was amazing!
He was sensational. He was a star!

Everyone was quiet listening to the
beautiful music of his voice. When he was
done, everyone exploded with applause.

"See?" exclaimed Patter. "I told you
he could sing!"

The besties began their dance.
They tapped their feet and paws, they

hopped forwards and backwards and they didn't make a single mistake. Twist thumped her paws. Caper swished her tail. Flick flicked her ears and Sprint tapped his hooves. Watching them, Flap couldn't resist. He wanted to dance, too! The peacock was ready to do the Bunny Bounce! He flapped off the perch and held on to Sprint's white tail. He spread his feathers and began hopping backwards and forwards. Fireflies landed on the tops of his long feathers and made them sparkle! He had never been so happy. He had friends and he was home at last.

Patter couldn't resist, either. She just had to sing. "La-la-la-la-LAAAA!" she squawked. "LA-LA-LA!"

Everyone covered their ears!

The moon was out. The stars were twinkling in the sky.

Patter and Flap were going to make everything in Wonderwood more colourful. A lot more colourful! The adventures of the Enchantimals had only just begun.

• • • ✿ • • •

F elicity stood back and stared at the
massive pile of stuff in the middle
of the room. The den where the fox-girl
lived with her bestie, Flick, was snug and
cosy. But the size of the pile made it seem
smaller than ever!

"What do you think, Flick?" she
asked. "Is that everything we need? Did
we forget anything?"

There was no answer.

"I just don't want to forget something

really important," Felicity continued. "Once you're in the wilderness, you can't just pop to a shop. You either improvise or you go without. Know what I mean?"

Flick still didn't respond.

Felicity paused. "Flick?" she called out. "Where are you?"

She stood very still, listening with all her might. Her pointed fox ears quivered as they tried to pick up the slightest sound. Then Felicity heard it: a faint *scritch-scratch-scritch* that could only be one thing. Flick was digging! Flick's little black paws had strong claws that were perfect for digging holes, tunnels and burrows.

But why would Flick be burrowing inside their cosy little den?

Suddenly, Felicity's hands flew to

her face as she gasped. "Flick! Are you digging out of the camping gear?" she exclaimed.

Scritch-scratch! Scratch-scritch!

The sound was coming from inside the pile of camping supplies.

Felicity's guess was correct!

"Don't worry, Flick!" she cried. "I'm on my way!"

The tents, the map, the compass, the canteen. Soon they were all flying through the air as Felicity tore through the pile to reach her bestie. At last, she saw it: Flick's small paw poking out of the pile.

"Gotcha!" Felicity exclaimed as she grabbed Flick's paw and pulled, pulled, pulled until Flick popped out of the pile. Felicity and Flick flew back and tumbled across the floor, finally coming to a landing on a soft, squishy stack of sleeping bags.

Felicity and Flick waggled their ears together, which was their special way of showing affection for each other.

"I'm sorry, Flick! I guess I got a little carried away with my packing. I didn't mean to cover you with all this stuff!"

"Uh-huh-huh!" Flick replied, letting Felicity know she forgave her.

"It's just that – well, you know – we've been planning this camping trip for ages and ages and I want everything to be just right!"